ADVENTURES IN THE KINGDOM™

THE DREAMER

Written by Dian Layton.
Illustrations created by Al Berg.

Moira

The King

Seeker

Glee

Gladness

Giggles

Do

Doodle

Yes

Dawdle

Slow

HopeSo

KnowSo

iii

Illustrations created by Al Berg.

Published by MercyPlace Ministries

MercyPlace is a licensed imprint of Destiny Image® Inc.

Distributed by

Destiny Image® Publishers, Inc.
P.O. Box 310
Shippensburg, PA 17257-0310

ISBN 0-9707919-4-1

For Worldwide Distribution
Printed in the U.S.A.

This book and all other Destiny Image, Revival Press, MercyPlace, Fresh Bread, Destiny Image Fiction, and Treasure House books are available at Christian bookstores and distributors worldwide.

For a U.S. bookstore nearest you, call **1-800-722-6774**.
For more information on foreign distributors, call **717-532-3040**.
Or reach us on the Internet: **www.seeker.org**

CONTENTS

CHAPTER ONE

"The World Beyond the Kingdom," Moira whispered, enjoying the sound of the words. "What a wonderful place it must be!"

The two charming visitors winked at each other knowingly and moved closer to Moira. Fantasy smiled as Trapper spoke with a voice that sounded as smooth as butter, "In the World Beyond the Kingdom," he said softly, "you can be who you want to be, and do what you want to do..."

Fantasy nodded. "And you can go where you want to go!" she said convincingly. "Just think, Moira—a place where you can make all your dreams come true!"

"Really?!" Moira responded hopefully, then flipped through the

magazines Trapper and Fantasy had given to her. The pages were filled with pictures of the shining buildings, tents and balloons and all the smiling faces of the people who lived there.

Trapper spoke again in his buttery voice, "You will meet Sophistication, Glamour, and Luxury, Moira. I promise. They are good friends of ours. And you will get to know True Happiness."

Fantasy looked at her watch and nodded. "Well, we need to run. We have an appointment with Opportunity right now!"

Moira waved good-bye and then started to walk toward her home in the Village of Peace and Harmony. The King's castle sparkled in the sunshine from its place on top of the hill. The Straight and Narrow Path stretched from the castle doors all the way down to the base of the hill and the Big Rock. That rock was a favorite meeting place for Moira's younger brother, Seeker, and his friends.

I hope Seeker isn't there today, Moira thought to herself. *I need to get home without having to answer any of his questions. Why should it matter to Seeker what I do with my time, anyway?*

Moira crossed the bridge into the Kingdom and was relieved to see that no one was at the Big Rock. She quickly turned toward the Village of Peace and Harmony. Maybe, just maybe, she would be lucky enough to get home before anyone noticed her.

Moira didn't realize that someone had noticed her. Seeker and some of his friends had watched her whole conversation with Trapper and Fantasy. As soon as Moira was out of hearing distance, Seeker, KnowSo, and Glee peeked out from behind the Big Rock. Then Dawdle and Slow peered out from behind them.

"See? I told you," Seeker said, shaking his head and sitting down on the rock.

"No wonder she hasn't been coming to the Adventure Club meetings lately," KnowSo said. "All the reasons she gave...I bet none of them were true..."

Glee sat on the rock beside Seeker. She was very upset. "I didn't believe you, Seeker," she whispered. "I still can hardly believe this is happening."

"Wh-Wh-Why wo-wo-would Moira g-g-go outside the Kingdom borders?" Dawdle and Slow asked together. "That's what I'd like to know," Seeker said. "I'd also like

3

to know the names of the people she was talking to. I've been thinking that maybe I should just go find them and tell them to leave my sister alone!"

KnowSo shook his head. "No—never do that, Seeker. I KNOW who they are."

"You do?" Seeker and Glee asked together.

KnowSo nodded. "I was reading about them in the King's library just last week. Their names are Trapper and Fantasy. They've been around for a very long time. Every day they walk near the Kingdom borders looking for children who are almost grown-up; people right around Moira's age."

"Why?" Seeker asked, his heart beating faster.

"They tell them lies about how much fun it would be to live in the World Beyond the Kingdom. They make the lies sound like the truth."

"M-M-Moira needs our help!" Dawdle said.

Slow nodded. "Wh-Wh-What can we do?" she asked.

"Should we tell the other kids?" KnowSo asked. "After all, Moira is a leader of the Adventure Club. The kids should know..."

Seeker shook his head. "Let's wait. I'll try talking to her tonight."

4

CHAPTER TWO

When Moira reached home, she took a deep breath and quietly opened the door...

"Moira, is that you?" her mother, Contentment, called out.

"Yeah, it's me," Moira answered, disappointed.

Contentment came around the corner with her gardening gloves on and dirt smudged across her face. "You're home rather late today, aren't you?" she asked. Moira shrugged, and Contentment pressed her a bit more. "Did you have a meeting after school?" she asked.

"Yeah, a meeting," Moira answered. "Now I've got homework to do."

"Do you have time to help me plant some new flowers?"

"Sorry, Mom," Moira said abruptly, going into her room.

Contentment stood looking at Moira's closed door and felt concern welling up in her heart. What was wrong with Moira? *It's not the door to her room that worries me,* Contentment thought. *But the door to her heart seems to be closing as well.*

Alone in her room, Moira shut her eyes and began to dance while singing her favorite song. It was a song she herself had written...

> *Hold a dream in your heart;*
> *Hold a castle, hold a rainbow*
> *Hold a picture, hold a promise, hold a prayer.*
> *For everything has a beginning;*
> *Mighty trees come from little seeds...*
> *And the desire in your heart*
> *for what might be—*
> *Will be—If you'll believe!*
> *So, hold a dream in your heart...*

Moira danced and danced and danced, then crumpled on the floor and leaned back against her bed. As she flipped through the magazines again, Trapper and Fantasy's words echoed in her mind. "Be who you want to be, go where you want to go, do what you want to do..."

A knock on the door made her jump up in surprise. Quickly, she hid the magazines and opened her school books. "Moira," Seeker called, "can I talk to you?"

"Not right now, Seeker! I'm busy!"

Seeker knocked again, louder this time. "Moira! PLEASE can I talk to you?"

Moira angrily stood up and opened the door just wide enough to see her brother's face. "What do you want?" she asked sharply. With a twinge of guilt she noticed Seeker's hurt expression, but she quickly brushed the feeling aside and spoke sharply again. "Well? What do you want?"

Seeker gulped and took a deep breath. "I want..." he said, "I want to know what is wrong with you lately! What's going on?"

"Nothing!" Moira snapped.

"Something is wrong! I know it is! You hardly ever come with us to the King's Celebration, and when you do come, you hardly eat anything and you never sing the songs!" Seeker pushed on the door and managed to squeeze through the opening into her room.

"What's it to you? Leave me alone, Seeker!"

"Moira! Don't you remember how you and I went to the Secret Place together and fought the dragons that were holding Dad prisoner? And what about the Adventure

7

Club? Doesn't it matter to you that we all miss you at the meetings?"

Moira felt herself begin to soften, then quickly hardened her heart again. "The Adventure Club is for you little kids! And the King would have gone to get Dad anyway—we didn't have anything to do with that! And we probably just imagined the dragons! Now get out of my room!" Moira pushed her brother into the hallway.

Seeker managed to block the door with his body before Moira had time to close it. "Wait! Moira, please! Talk to me! What's wrong? Maybe I can help..."

Moira's eyes flashed in anger. "How could you help? You're just a kid! And there's nothing wrong, anyway! Just leave me alone!"

This time she managed to slam the door and Seeker was left standing in the hallway. He leaned close to the door and said, "Moira, if you won't let me help, why not go to the King? He REALLY wants to talk to you...I saw him watching you at school the other day! Why not go, just once, and..."

"No!" Moira opened the door unexpectedly and he nearly fell into the room. "Listen, Seeker, you can't spend your whole life running to the King about every little thing! There comes a time when a person just has to grow up and make some decisions on their own! That's all I'm doing—making some decisions! Now will you please just leave me alone?!!" With that she slammed the door again.

"Okay, Moira," Seeker whispered through the door. "I'll go now. But whatever is wrong, whatever is making you so upset, I REALLY know that the King can help you. Good night."

Moira leaned against the door and waited, listening as Seeker's footsteps went down the hall to his room. She listened to the sound of his door opening and then softly closing.

The ache in her heart felt unbearable. "Seeker's right," she whispered to herself. "There is something wrong with me! Why do I hurt so much inside?"

Moira knew that she should be happy. After all, her father had returned to the Kingdom after being away for more than two years. The King had rescued him from Despair and changed his name from Wanderer to Steadfast. Lately, Contentment had been visiting Steadfast in the castle where he was living, and they were talking about the possibility of his moving back home again. *I should be so happy!* Moira thought. *Why am I so miserable?*

Moira sat down on the bed beside her school books and thumbed through her math assignment where she had sketched pictures of the World Beyond the Kingdom instead of math equations. It had been so hard to concentrate on school work lately...

In the King's castle was a special tower where the children of the Kingdom went to school. They learned math and science and spelling...and they also learned about the King and his Kingdom. During class time, the King often came to visit the students.

Moira had become more and more uncomfortable when the King came into the classroom. She often looked up from her books to find him watching her. He seemed to be calling to her, "Moira, come and spend some time with me. Moira, let's talk."

In fact, earlier that week, the King had slipped a note into her bag. It was a royal invitation. Sitting there on her bed, Moira opened the envelope and read it again.

Dear Moira,
Please come and talk to me.
Call to me and I will always answer you.
Love forever,
The King

"No!" Moira whispered. "I can't talk to the King! This is my last year in the school. I'm almost grown up now...what if the King has plans for me—who he wants me to be, where he wants me to go, what he wants me to do, and...what if the King's plans for me are totally different from my dreams?"

Moira shut her eyes tightly as a flood of thoughts raced around in her mind...Trapper and Fantasy's stories, the King's invitation, Seeker's pleading voice...until, totally exhausted, she finally fell asleep. And while she slept, Moira dreamed about pink balloons and shining buildings in the World Beyond the Kingdom.

CHAPTER THREE

"How could you help? You're just a kid!"

Moira's sharp words from the night before echoed in Seeker's mind as he awoke the next morning. *Just a kid?* he thought. *Just a kid?! Well, around here in the Kingdom, little can be very big! I think it's about time the kids of the Kingdom marched as an army again!*

Seeker jumped out of bed, dressed, ran downstairs, ate some breakfast, and headed toward the door. "Oops! Forgot about my teeth!" Usually Seeker's mother was standing at the door, smiling and holding his toothbrush. But today Seeker realized the house was strangely quiet.

14

"Mom?" he called. "Moira? Hey, where is everybody?"

Seeker found his mother in her garden—pulling unusually hard at some weeds that had secured themselves into the ground. She seemed upset and Seeker hesitated about interrupting her.

"Weeds, Seeker," Contentment spoke, knowing that he was watching her. "We need to get rid of the weeds or they will choke out the good plants and all these beautiful flowers."

With her eyes brimming with tears, Contentment looked at her son. "Our hearts are like a garden." Tears slipped out and down her cheeks. "Your sister's heart...is like a garden..."

Seeker moved to kneel beside his mother, putting an arm reassuringly around her shoulders. "A flower garden, Mom, just like yours. She'll be okay, you'll see."

Contentment shook her head. "She's gone, Seeker."

Seeker felt like his heart stopped beating. "Gone? What do you mean, gone?"

"Moira left sometime during the night. She left this note for us." Contentment pulled a tear-stained paper from her pocket and read aloud. "Dear Mom and Seeker, you know how hard it's been for me in the Kingdom lately and I've made my decision. I thought about it a lot and feel like this is what I need to do..."

15

Contentment's voice broke and she handed the note to Seeker to continue reading. "I'm not sure where I'm going except that I'm going to make my dreams come true. Please don't try to find me. I'll write you a letter when I get settled. I still love you and I'm sorry that I have to do this. Moira."

Seeker stood up, determination filling his heart. "The King will know what to do, Mom! He will go and get Moira and bring her home, I just know it! I'm going for help!"

Seeker hurried through the gate and raced through the streets of Peace and Harmony, calling to his friends,

16

"Emergency meeting in the King's Throne Room! Right away!" he shouted as he ran past their homes.

HopeSo, KnowSo and Yes; Giggles, Gladness, and Glee; Doodle and Do hurried out of their houses and followed close behind Seeker. Dawdle and Slow struggled to keep up. "Wh-wh-what's wrong, Seeker?" Dawdle called.

"I-I-Is M-M-Moira okay, Seeker?" Slow asked, running as fast as her legs would carry her.

With panting sentences, Seeker explained about Moira's note as he led his friends past the Big Rock and up the Straight and Narrow Path to the castle.

The Doorkeeper didn't stop the children with his usual question, "Do you REALLY want to see the King?" Instead, he quickly opened the door just in time for the army of children to race through. They slid down the shining hallway—not for fun today, but just because it was faster than walking—and flung themselves through the door of the Throne Room.

The King was standing there, as though he had been expecting them.

"King, King!" Seeker cried out. "Moira left the Kingdom!"

"I know," the King said quietly.

"She was gone when Mom and I got up this morning!" Seeker hurried on, not aware that the King had answered him.

"I know," the King repeated.

Finally, Seeker realized what the King had said. "You KNOW?!" he exclaimed, "Then why don't you do something?! King, you just have to go and get her!"

The King quietly shook his head. "No, Seeker, not until she really wants me to. Come, let's go out to the courtyard."

As they walked outside, Glee pleaded with the King, "Please, King! We love Moira!"

18

"Yes!" Yes agreed, taking the King's hand. "We REAL-LY love her! Please go and get her!"

"D-D-Don't worry," Dawdle said reassuringly. "The K-K-King will l-l-look after Moira."

Slow looked up at the King, her eyes wide with trust, and said, "W-W-Won't you, King?!"

Seeker was frantic. "King! You just have to go and get her and make her come back!"

The King shook his head. "No. Not until she really wants me to." The King smiled gently at Seeker and his friends. "But there is something that all of you can do for Moira...something that will really help her."

"What, King?" the children asked hopefully.

"Spend time in the Secret Place. Talk to me every day about Moira."

(The Secret Place is a special place where people can go and talk to the King about how they feel. They don't always see him, but he is always there!)

"Okay!" Seeker said. "We'll talk to you in the Secret Place. And what about us marching as a army, King? Like when we defeated the dragon Greed!"

19

"Yeah, let's DO it!" Doodle said enthusiastically. "We can be your army again, King! We can go and rescue Moira from...from..." he paused, seeing Seeker's horrified expression.

"Dragons," Seeker whispered. "I never even thought about dragons! King! Are there dragons after Moira?"

The King put his arm around Seeker's shoulders to comfort him. "Dragons sent messengers to speak to Moira and she listened to their voices."

"Trapper and Fantasy," KnowSo nodded knowingly.

"But no dragons will be able to touch Moira if you stand guard," the King said, looking at the anxious young faces around him. "In the Secret Place, you can be my army; my very big little army. Moira will be protected." The King paused for a moment, then continued, "I will be watching her. The moment she calls to me, I will answer her!"

"Okay, King," Seeker said and his friends nodded their agreement. "We will spend time every day in the Secret Place!"

"We will DO it!" Doodle and Do announced together.

CHAPTER FOUR

Weeks and months passed, and whenever Seeker wasn't with his friends in the Secret Place, he spent time helping Contentment in her flower garden. On one such day, Seeker took a deep breath and said, "Mom, this place smells so good! I just love coming here!"

Contentment smiled and sat down, wiping her brow with a happy sigh. "It is nice, isn't it? It's my Secret Place..."

"Your Secret Place?" echoed Seeker.

"Yes. I love talking with the King while I work in this garden. It helps me to remember that the garden he is most interested in is right in here." Contentment pointed to her heart.

"My Secret Place is in one of the towers of the castle," Seeker said, as he sat down beside Contentment. "My friends and I have been going there every day to talk to the King about Moira. He said that if we would do that, she would be protected."

Contentment nodded. "As I talk to the King here in my garden, I sometimes feel as though I am working in the garden of Moira's heart. I'm planting good seeds...and someday soon those seeds will prove stronger than the weeds that Moira allowed to grow."

"Weeds," Seeker said thoughtfully. "Is that why she left the Kingdom, Mom? What kind of weeds?"

"I've tried to name some of them as I pull weeds out of this garden," Contentment said. "I think the main weeds in Moira's heart were Guilt, Anger, and Silence."

Seeing Seeker's wondering expression, Contentment continued, "I think the weeds entered Moira's heart around the time your father became Wanderer and lived in Despair. Moira felt guilty because she thought that somehow she should have been able to stop your dad from leaving us."

"That's not true!" Seeker exclaimed. "Dad made that choice—Moira had nothing to do with it! That's a lie!"

"Believing lies is how the weeds begin, Seeker," Contentment explained. "Then Moira allowed anger to creep into her heart. She kept silent about how she was

really feeling...and that silence made it easier for the weeds to take root."

"Silence...She never talked to you?" asked Seeker.

"She didn't talk to me," Contentment answered, "and I'm fairly sure that she didn't talk to the King, either. I mean really talk to him—you know, about how she was feeling inside."

Suddenly, Seeker sat up straight and exclaimed, "Oh no! I just remembered something that happened back when the Adventure Club first began! We all went with the King to the underground passageway between Royal Harbor and the castle. The King was teaching us about not living in Darkness; and that day he asked Moira to come and talk to him about how she was really feeling..."

"And did she do that?" Contentment asked.

Seeker shook his head. "I don't think so. She and I began to go to my Secret Place together and we talked to the King about Dad...but I don't think that Moira ever had a Secret Place of her own...No wonder the King looked so worried about her that day!"

Contentment sighed. "She seemed to be close to the King...I just assumed that she was talking to him about her feelings. It's so important to do that!" Contentment reached inside her apron pocket where she always carried a copy of the King's Great Book. "Here, Seeker, let me show you something..." She flipped through the pages until she came to the place she was looking for.

"Pour out your heart to the King," she read aloud. "He is a very present help in times of trouble." Contentment closed the book and held it to her heart. "If Moira would have poured out her feelings to the King, those feelings would have been healed..."

"And the weeds would have been pulled out of her garden, before they really took root," Seeker said.

Contentment stood up and said, " During the past few days as I've worked, a new song has been growing in my heart, Seeker. Would you like to hear it?"

Seeker nodded quickly. His mom was great at making up songs! She sang it thorough once, then Seeker joined in. The song was so much fun that Contentment and Seeker danced around the garden with a hoe and rake as they sang...

My heart is a garden
Where the King goes walkin'
And I want him to like it there...
I want the bushes and the flowers
To really overpower
Any little weeds still there...
And I'll pull out things like worry or anger
Before they can start to take root
And I'll plant the seeds of kindness and forgiveness
To keep my heart shining and new!

I won't listen to lies—that always seem to try
To take my attention from the truth!
And if my heart becomes overcome
With sadness—here's what I know I should do –
I run to the King and I pour my heart out
I tell him my troubles and fears

'Cause—my heart is a garden
Where the King goes walkin'
And I want him to like it here...

"Wonderful!" said the King as he clapped and smiled from the entrance of the flower garden.

Contentment and Seeker turned toward him and bowed low in delighted surprise. "Your Majesty!"

Seeker ran to hug him. "Hi, King!"

The King smiled a bigger smile and said, "Hi." Then he reached out his hands to Seeker and Contentment. "Come," said the King, "I will show you what happened in this garden while you sang!"

Contentment and Seeker looked at each other, wondering. What could have happened while they sang? They walked with the King to the far corner of the flower garden. There, beside a strong fruit tree, was a fountain. It was bubbling with crystal clear water that flowed out into a sparkling little pond.

"Wow!" said Seeker. "Where did that come from?"

"From my castle," said the King. "The water in that fountain is the same water that flows out from my throne room..."

"It's beautiful, King!" Contentment said as she hugged him. "Thank you!"

Seeker watched his mother with a new sense of appreciation. *All that she has been through,* Seeker thought to himself, *all the problems with Dad...and now*

28

the problems with Moira...but Mom just keeps spending time here in her Secret Place; and no weeds like anger or worry can grow inside her.

Seeker leaned against a rock near the fountain and his thoughts again turned toward his sister. *If only Moira would find a Secret Place and talk to the King...*

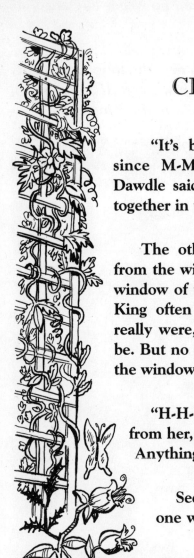

CHAPTER FIVE

"It's b-b-been a v-v-very long time since M-M-Moira l-left the Kingdom," Dawdle said one day as the children met together in the Secret Place.

The others nodded and turned away from the window, feeling discouraged. The window of the Secret Place was where the King often showed them the way things really were, not the way they appeared to be. But no pictures had been seen through the window for a long time.

"H-H-Have you h-h-heard any thing from her, S-S-Seeker?" asked Slow, "...A-Anything at all?"

Seeker shook his head. "No. Not one word. All this waiting is so hard!

30

I've been wondering if there isn't something we could be doing to help Moira."

Doodle and Do agreed excitedly. "Great idea! Let's DO something!"

"Yes!" Yes exclaimed. "I mean, after all, we ARE the King's army! There must be something we can do to help Moira!"

The other children stood at attention and saluted. They were the King's army! Ready for battle!

KnowSo shook his head and motioned for them to relax. "You KNOW we can't do anything until the King gives the orders," he said.

"Okay, okay," said Seeker. "But today, I'm going to REALLY ask the King if there's something we could be doing!"

Glee had been quietly looking through the window of the Secret Place while her friends talked; but now she exclaimed, "I just saw a picture!"

"A picture?" Giggles echoed as everyone gathered around Glee. "What was it?" The children peered through the window intently, but no one could see a picture except Glee.

"A map!" she exclaimed. "Yes, I think it's a map."

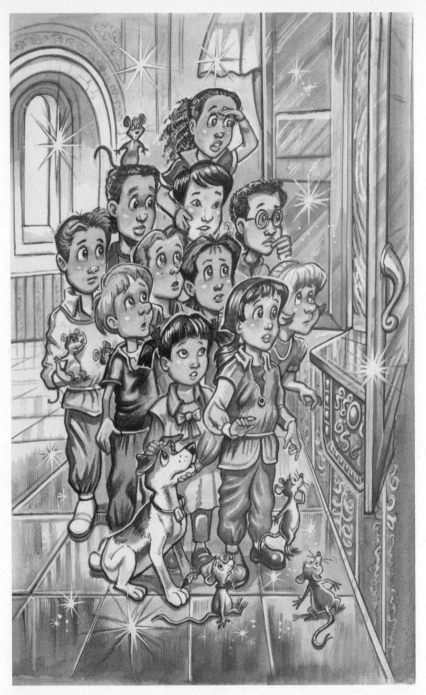

Doodle reached inside his pocket for a pencil and paper. "Tell us what it looks like and I'll try to draw it!"

Glee peered again through the window. "Okay...I can see the castle...and the bridge. Past that is the World Beyond the Kingdom..."

"The World Beyond the Kingdom?" Seeker echoed excitedly. "That's where Moira is!"

"I KNOW!" KnowSo said. "Maybe the King is showing us the exact place where Moira is so that we can go and get her!"

Everyone gathered around Glee. "Look harder," Do said. "What DO you see now?"

Glee squinted her eyes, struggling to see. Everyone held their breath in anticipation, but then she shook her head. "Sorry. That's all there is."

"M-M-Maybe," Dawdle said, "the m-map isn't for us."

"What do you mean?" the others wanted to know.

"M-M-Maybe the map is for Moira," Dawdle said, "M-M-Maybe she can't find her way back home."

"I know what we'll DO," cried Do excitedly. "Doodle can draw a map for Moira and we'll send it to her!"

The others stared at Do with blank expressions. "D-D-DO you have her address?" Slow asked.

"Oh, uh, well, no," stuttered Do. "I guess that was a really dumb idea, huh?"

Seeker came to his friend's rescue. "No, it was a great idea!"

"DO you really think so?" Do asked hopefully.

"Yes!" Seeker said. "Listen, we can send the map to Moira—we can ask the King to take it to her!"

"How?"

"In a dream," Seeker said intensely. "Moira was always talking about her dreams! Let's ask the King to send her a dream—a dream that would help her find her way back home!"

"Okay!" shouted Do. "Let's DO it!"

As the children joined hands in the Secret Place, Seeker shut his eyes tightly and whispered, "Wherever she is right now...send her a dream, King. Help Moira find her way back home."

"Y-Y-Yes, King," said Dawdle and Slow, "and wh-wh-wherever she is, protect her..."

CHAPTER SIX

"Help! Please someone, help me!"

The voice of a young woman cried out from a dark alley and a moment later she was thrown down some worn steps where she landed in a pool of mud. Two men stood in the doorway.

"That'll teach you!" one man roared. The second man angrily pointed his finger at her. "Who do you think you are, anyway? Now get out of here before we really hurt you!"

The young woman struggled to her feet and pushed her matted hair away from her eyes.

It was Moira.

Trembling from the close call she had just had with Anger and Jealousy, Moira wrapped her coat around her thin body and hurried down the alley. "Whew," she whispered. "Anger was just about to strike me when for some reason he stopped! That was scary."

When she reached a dimly lit street, Moira paused to rest. Some of Anger's words echoed in her mind. "Who do you think you are, anyway?" Over and over again the phrase repeated, "Who do you think you are, anyway?"

That's a very good question, Moira thought. *Who am I?* As Moira sat there, the deepest longings of her heart took the shape of a song, and she sang it softly...

Who am I? Why am I?
Where am I going?
Won't someone show me the way?
Who am I? Why am I?
Where am I going?
Won't someone show me the way?
I used to have a dream inside of my heart –
A vision and a promise filled with hope...
But now those dreams and visions
They've all shattered
And nothing seems to matter anymore.
How I used to dream
Of the person I would be.
How I used to dream of the people
I would meet.
How I used to...dream...

Suddenly, Moira realized that someone was watching her, listening to her song. A tall, slender woman moved quietly across the street and stood beside Moira.

"Who are you?" Moira whispered.

"My name is Loneliness," came the soft reply. "I heard you singing. You sounded like you needed a friend. Can I walk with you for a while?"

Moira smiled and nodded, "Thanks, yes, I'd like that. I really do need a friend..."

Loneliness seemed right at home in the dark pathways Moira chose and as they walked together, Moira told Loneliness everything that had happened since she had come to live in the World Beyond the Kingdom...

Moira's story was one that Loneliness had heard before but she listened compassionately as Moira spoke.

For awhile, life in the World seemed to be everything Moira had expected it to be. Trapper and Fantasy introduced her to many people. She met Sophistication and made friends with Glamour and Luxury. Although she never got to know True Happiness, Moira went places, and did things, and felt as though she was on her way to having all her dreams come true.

But...

As the weeks and months passed Moira discovered that the World Beyond the Kingdom was not what she had expected it to be, after all. The buildings that looked shiny were dull and dreary inside. The pink balloons she had dreamed about did not exist. The farther she got from the Kingdom, the darker it became, and the people Moira had thought were her friends were not her friends after all.

Trapper and Fantasy moved away to a different city without telling Moira where they went.

Glamour became Emptiness. Luxury became Poverty, and Moira learned that Sophistication's real name was Charade.

For a few short weeks, Moira had thought she had met True Happiness but then discovered that the person was wearing a mask and was actually Anger. That's who had thrown her out onto the street a few hours earlier.

As Moira finished telling Loneliness her story, she shivered again with a mixture of fear and relief. "He was about to strike me. He was so angry! But then, for some reason, he just threw me out of the door!"

"Someone was watching out for you," Loneliness said softly.

Moira was startled. "Someone was watching out for me?" she repeated. "But no one even knows where I am! And no one would care enough, anyway." An uncomfortable ache came into Moira's heart and she tried to ignore it.

"So, Loneliness," she said, "what about you? Tell me about yourself."

But Loneliness didn't answer. She just pulled her coat closer to her face for warmth and they kept walking.

CHAPTER SEVEN

More time went by while Moira explored
the World Beyond the Kingdom, still hoping
that somehow all of her dreams would hap-
pen. But the farther she got from the
Kingdom, the darker her life became.
Several times, Moira was sure that she had
seen dragons peering out from their hiding
places along her path; but still she continued
on, hoping that around the next corner she
might meet Opportunity, or perhaps she
might find True Happiness, as Trapper and
Fantasy had promised.

But, after months and months of
searching, Moira found herself in a sad and
miserable place called "The Valley of Lost
Dreams" with Loneliness as her constant
companion. The only sound was the dis-
tant bleating of sheep in a pasture.

Much of the time Moira and Loneliness spent together was spent in silence, each thinking their own troubled, lonely thoughts. Although Loneliness rarely spoke, Moira learned that she had a young son. The few times Loneliness mentioned him, her eyes filled with sorrow and she would whisper, "So many regrets. So many regrets..." Then she would grow silent again and refuse to answer Moira's questions.

One morning, Moira said to Loneliness, "I had a dream last night."

Loneliness turned to her with interest. Dreams were very, very rare in that valley.

"I dreamed I was lost in a garden," Moira said.

Loneliness came and sat closer, and Moira continued, "It was very dark and the garden was overgrown with weeds. The harder I tried to find my way out, the more lost I became, and I got tangled up in the weeds." Moira shivered remembering.

"And then what happened?" Loneliness asked.

"My brother, Seeker...he came to me in the garden and handed me a map...At least, I thought it was a map;

42

but then, when I looked at it, it was actually the words and music of a song."

Moira stood up, suddenly excited as she remembered more details of the dream. "Yes, it was a song, but not just any song! It was a song that I myself wrote a very long time ago. I had forgotten all about it! The words are: Hold a dream in your heart..." Moira paused, then remembered more of the words, "Hold a castle, hold a rainbow...Hold a picture, hold a promise, hold a prayer..."

The words bubbled up inside Moira and although she couldn't remember the melody, she began to dance around just like she used to dance in her room at night...

After a few moments of dancing and struggling to bring the song back to her mind, Moira became aware that Loneliness was watching her with a look of deep pity.

"You don't believe me!" Moira said in surprise as she stopped dancing. "You think I'm just making it all up, don't you?"

Loneliness shook her head but Moira continued, "Well it's true! I did have dreams! Lots and lots of wonderful dreams!"

Loneliness again looked at Moira with deep pity. "I'm so sorry," she whispered. "I'm so sorry you've lost your dreams, Moira. I'm so sorry you've forgotten the song. Maybe if you tried again to remember...maybe if you thought some more about the dream that you had last night..."

Moira nodded and smiled feebly at Loneliness. "Okay. I'll try."

She shut her eyes and thought again about the paper Seeker had handed to her in the dream. Suddenly, Moira could see it just as clearly as when she dreamed it...but now, the paper no longer held words and music. Instead, on the paper was a picture of the King...and there, beneath his picture, were the words of the invitation he had given to her so long ago.

Moira's eyes shot open and she stood up so suddenly that Loneliness was startled. It had been such a long time since Moira had thought about the King. The expression on his face in the picture was exactly the same as when he used to look at her. "I wonder what he wanted to say to me?" she asked aloud.

"Who?" asked Loneliness.

"Someone I used to know," answered Moira. "Someone very wonderful. He wanted me to come and talk to him, but...but I was afraid."

Loneliness nodded. "Fear keeps people from doing what they later wish they would have done; or else it makes them do things they wish they would not have done." Loneliness's voice dropped to a whisper and her eyes filled with deep sorrow. "Regrets. So many regrets..."

44

Moira took hold of her friend's hands and spoke earnestly. "I wish I would have gone to see him...just once ...just once! Why didn't I do that?" Moira's voice trailed off and she dropped Loneliness's hands. "Oh well, it's too late now. He's probably really angry with me for leaving the Kingdom, and even if I wanted to go back, it's too far. I'd never find my way."

"The Kingdom?" asked Loneliness. "You were in a Kingdom?" When Moira nodded, Loneliness spoke hopefully. "And a King...is there really a King? I heard about him once but...is he real?"

Moira nodded again, and dug through her bag, searching. "Here it is—the King's invitation! I could never bring myself to throw it away." She handed it to Loneliness, who opened the envelope carefully and read aloud:

Dear Moira,
Please come and talk to me.
Call to me and I will always answer you.
Love forever,
The King

Loneliness looked up, her eyes wide. "An invitation from the King. A personal letter from him! Oh, Moira..."

Tears welled up in Moira's eyes, and she nodded. "Yes. A personal invitation from the King, and I ignored it!" She wiped the tears away and then continued with an intensity Loneliness had never heard before. "If I had the chance, I would do things differently. I never would have

45

left the Kingdom! I promise I would have stayed there! If only the King would give me another chance. If only it wasn't too late!"

At that very moment, Moira heard a sound. She looked up. There, in the meadow across from the Valley of Lost Dreams, was a lamb. It was the saddest looking little lamb that Moira had ever seen. It was struggling through the grass, tripping, falling, and crying out in pain and confusion.

"Oh, the poor thing!" Moira exclaimed to Loneliness. "It must have gotten out from the pasture somehow! I wonder what we can do to help it?"

But before either Moira or Loneliness could think of a way to help the lamb, a shepherd came. He stepped out from the thick forest near the Valley of Lost Dreams and walked over to where the crumpled little heap of wool had fallen. The shepherd bent down and gently picked up the lamb in his strong arms, and holding it very closely, carried it away.

Tears spilled out and over Moira's cheeks as she watched. "That's me," she whispered. "I'm just like that lamb. That's me! Oh, Loneliness, I'm so lost and so scared and oh, I really wish I had a second chance!" Moira fell down to her knees, crying.

Loneliness gently touched Moira's shoulder and pointed. There, coming toward them, was the shepherd. He walked swiftly and purposefully, as though he had something important to do.

Moira quickly wiped the tears away. They weren't used to visitors coming to the Valley. "I wonder what he wants," she said.

"Perhaps," Loneliness whispered to Moira with a tender smile, "perhaps he is looking for another lost lamb."

Loneliness shyly stepped back as the shepherd approached. He stood silently for a moment in front of Moira, and then, very slowly, the shepherd pushed back the hood of his cloak.

It was...the King.

Moira gasped with surprise. The King! What was he doing here in the Valley of Lost Dreams? What did he think of her being in such a place? Shame and embarrassment washed through Moira like a wave. She held her head low and turned away, silently asking the King to leave her. But the King did not leave. Instead, he bent down to the place where Moira was, gently picked her in up in his strong arms, and held her closely, just like he had held the little lamb.

And then, ever so softly, the King began to sing...

Hold a dream in your heart
Hold a castle, hold a rainbow
Hold a picture, Hold a promise
Hold a prayer...

Moira was amazed. "King! King, that's the song I used to sing! I was trying to remember the tune…!" Moira broke off, suddenly confused. "But…I wrote that song! Where did you learn it?"

The King held her even closer. "Moira," he whispered gently, "I was the one who put that song in your heart!"

Then the King began to tell Moira about the dreams he had for her life—who he wanted her to be, where he wanted her to go, and what he wanted her to do.

And they were her dreams!

"My dreams," she whispered, as they poured back into her heart like a flood. Cheerful dreams, big dreams, plans and visions for the future tumbled through her mind one after the other like a joyful parade. "My dreams are back! But now they are brighter and even more wonderful than before!"

Moira shut here eyes tightly, watching the happy thoughts in her mind. As she watched, she saw some of the dream from the night before. She was in a garden, but the tangled weeds were gone. Flowering plants, just beginning to bud, lined a pathway. In the center of the garden was a golden bench, and on the bench sat the King. His expression was the same one she had seen so many times before. He was calling to her, "Come and talk to me. Call to me and I will always answer you…"

Moira's eyes shot open in realization. She knew what it was he wanted to talk to her about...it was her future! The King wanted to talk to her about the dreams that he himself had placed in her heart. She had never needed to fear the King's plans for her; what she needed to do was to get close to him!

The King smiled at Moira, seeing the light of understanding in her eyes. He stood to his feet, still holding her in his great arms. "Let's go home," he said.

As they headed back toward the Kingdom, away from the Valley of Lost Dreams, Moira nestled deeper into the King's arms. *He's not angry!* she thought. *He came all this way just to get me; he has plans, dreams for my life— dreams that now seem even more wonderful than before!*

Love for the King welled up inside her heart like a garden of flowers ready to burst into bloom. Moira impulsively threw her arms around the King's neck and hugged him really tight.

The King laughed...and his laughter filled the whole valley....

Back in the Kingdom, Seeker and his friends had been watching through the window of the Secret Place.

"Hooray!" everyone shouted as they hugged Seeker. "Moira's coming home! Moira's coming home!"

After a few moments of happy celebrating, the children hurried out from the Secret Place and raced down the Straight and Narrow path toward the Big Rock. They wanted to be there when the King and Moira arrived.

"I'll be right back," Seeker shouted. "I'm going to get Mom!"

None of the children noticed that two of their friends weren't with them. They didn't realize that Dawdle and Slow were still looking through the window, tears falling silently down their cheeks. "I-I'm happy for M-Moira," Dawdle said.

"B-But what about L-L-Loneliness?" asked Slow.

Dawdle and Slow watched Loneliness huddled on a bench and shivering in the cool air; and they watched the King. Just before he and Moira left the Valley of Lost Dreams, the King turned back toward the lonely young woman. He looked at her intently and smiled a mysterious smile. Then the King looked directly through the window of the Secret Place, right at Dawdle and Slow. He leaned forward slightly and winked at them.

A wave of delighted relief washed through the two children. "Th-The King has a pl-pl-plan for L-Loneliness!" Dawdle cried excitedly.

Slow nodded happily. "H-He's not going to l-l-leave her in Lost Dreams!"

And then Dawdle and Slow hurried from the Secret Place as fast as they were able. They wanted to be there to welcome Moira back to the Kingdom of Joy and Peace.

Land of Laws Forgotten

Island of Despair

ROYAL HARBOR

GENEROSITY

CARNALVILLE

Valley of Lost Dreams

Talking Tree Forest

The Kingdom of Joy and Peace

World Beyond the Kingdom

N
E   W
S

53

THINK ABOUT THE STORY

Perhaps you have wonderful dreams in your heart about the future. Jesus Christ is the King of all kings. He has a dream for your life. Have you ever asked Him what it is?

Or perhaps you used to know His dreams, but you've been wandering away. If you are in the Valley of Lost Dreams, call out to the King! He will pick you up, heal your wounds, and rekindle the dream in your heart.

SEARCH THE PAGES OF THE KING'S GREAT BOOK...

Ephesians 3:20 - You can never dream too big a dream!
Jeremiah 29:11 - His plans for you are GOOD.
Proverbs 16:25 - Careful! There is a pathway that looks right, but it's not!

TALK TO THE KING...

"Hi, King. Sometimes people ask me what I'm going to do when I grow up. I need to ask YOU that question! There are lots and lots of things I can plan and think about doing. Please help me to spend my time seeking YOU about my future. The world beyond Your Kingdom looks attractive, but I know that the dreams that You put into my heart will only come true as I stay in Your Kingdom, close to You."

VERSES TO REMEMBER...

I must have a vision,
a plan from the King—
Or I will end up living carelessly.
Proverbs 29:18—
May HIS dreams come true in me! (H.W.P.)

The King is able to do–
Exceeding, abundantly–
Above all I ask or think—
ACCORDING TO HIS POWER IN ME!
Ephesians chapter 3 and verse 20—
Dream big dreams, everybody!

Adventures in the Kingdom™
by Dian Layton

— SEEKER'S GREAT ADVENTURE

Seeker and his friends leave the CARNALville of Selfishness and begin the great adventure of really knowing the King!

— RESCUED FROM THE DRAGON

The King needs an army to conquer a very disgusting dragon and rescue the people who live in the Village of Greed.

— SECRET OF THE BLUE POUCH

The children of the Kingdom explore the pages of an ancient golden book and step through a most remarkable doorway — into a brand new kind of adventure!

— IN SEARCH OF WANDERER

Come aboard the sailing ship *The Adventurer*, and find out how Seeker learns to fight dragons through the window of the Secret Place.

— THE DREAMER

Moira, Seeker's older sister, leaves the Kingdom and disappears into the Valley of Lost Dreams. Can Seeker rescue his sister before it's too late?

— ARMOR OF LIGHT

In the World Beyond the Kingdom, Seeker must use the King's weapons to fight the dragons Bitterness and Anger to save the life of one young boy.

— CARRIERS OF THE KINGDOM

Seeker and his friends discover that the Kingdom is within them! In the Land of Laws Forgotten they meet with Opposition, and the children battle against some very nasty dragons who do not want the people to remember...

Available at your local Christian bookstore.

For more information and sample chapters, visit www.destinyimage.com or www.seeker.org

Now Join Seeker

& His Friends

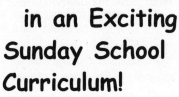

in an Exciting
Sunday School
Curriculum!

Learn New
Things
About the
King and Get
to Know Him
Better
at
Seeker.org

Check out Seeker.org
or Call
1.800.722.6774

The Young God Chasers
Curriculum Series by Dian Layton

Seeking the King

(With quotes and concepts from *The God Chasers* by Tommy Tenney) Many children who attend church "live in the Kingdom, but don't know the King." A God Chaser is a "SEEKER"! The lessons in this first binder are designed to encourage hunger in the children's hearts to really KNOW (not just know ABOUT) King Jesus!

The King and His Kingdom

(With quotes and concepts from *The God Chasers* by Tommy Tenney) Children need to hear what is on the King's heart and then DO what He tells them to do...not just "some day when they grow up"; but NOW! Children can be part of His "very big little army" and have a powerful impact on the world around them!

Seeker's Sources of Power

(With quotes and concepts from *Secret Sources of Power* by Tommy Tenney) The concept of having POWER is intriguing to children. How valuable for youngsters to learn that the true source of power is being emptied of self and filled up with Jesus! They will learn how to live a POWER-FILLED life every day!

Seeker's Secret Place

(With quotes and concepts from *Secret Sources of Power* by Tommy Tenney) Many people spend time in counseling sessions trying to get free of the guilt, worry, fear, and sin they have been carrying around for years. In this curriculum, children learn how to "cast all their cares" and "unload their heavy burdens" on Jesus.

Watch for these titles at your local Christian bookstore.